THE SKY-RIDERS

THE SKY-RIDERS

BY PAUL DELLINGER AND MIKE ALLEN

Mythic Delirium
BOOKS

mythicdelirium.com

The Sky-Riders

Published by Mythic Delirium Books

mythicdelirium.com

Our gratitude goes out to the following who because of their generosity are from now on designated as supporters of Mythic Delirium Books: Saira Ali, Cora Anderson, Anonymous, Patricia M. Cryan, Steve Dempsey, Oz Drummond, Patrick Dugan, Matthew Farrer, C. R. Fowler, Mary J. Lewis, Paul T. Muse, Jr., Shyam Nunley, Finny Pendragon, Kenneth Schneyer, and Delia Sherman.

PAUL'S DEDICATION:

For Grace and Emma: The sky's the limit.

MIKE'S DEDICATION:

For Mom: A dashing bit of derring-do!

Table of Contents

ONE

The Oddest Sight

Alistair Jones pulled his gray gelding to a halt, rising in his stirrups to peer down into a valley at what must be the oddest sight this part of the world had seen since John Wesley Hardin caught his pistol in his suspenders trying to outdraw a Texas Ranger.

"Dusty, just what the hell is that?" he asked the horse. Dusty's eyes had widened and his nostrils flared, but he ventured no opinion.

Man and horse stared down at what looked to be a gigantic gray hump jouncing along behind a ridge. Jones might have thought it to be some hitherto unclassified frontier animal, even though he figured the American frontier had been pretty well explored by now, three years before the 19th century would be relegated to the history books. But the two rows of metallic wheel-like objects on thick poles along its sides, glowing and steaming in the northeastern Texas sunlight, had to be man-made. Whatever those were, Jones knew they were nothing birthed by nature.

He kept gawking as the ridge ahead of the behemoth began to dip and it moved more into the open. Now he could make out more of its shape. It reminded him of a colossal pillow, or maybe a fat monster cigar, its sides seeming to breathe in and out as though maybe it really was alive. But then the ridge dropped further and a wagon came into view beneath the thing, if you could call it a wagon. It had wheels, three sets of them, and was longer than any wagon he'd ever seen. It was being pulled by a team of only six mules, so its burden couldn't be as heavy as its size would indicate.

Those mules were moving at a pretty good clip, but Jones saw they would have to stop soon because the valley was narrowing and they were running out of space. Apparently the driver realized this at the same time as Jones, because he could now see the man, dwarfed by the size of the wagon, hauling back on the reins and applying the brake with his foot. Jones saw three other men jump down from the wagon and take cover in the rocks around it.

Then Jones saw why they had been in a hurry.

A half-dozen riders emerged from behind the ridge in obvious pursuit and, at least from this distance, it seemed to Jones that they all looked alike. For one thing, they all seemed rather rotund in their matching black coats and trousers. Even from up here, he could see that they all wore black bowler hats—not that those were uncommon, having been the hat of choice for celebrated westerners from Bat Masterson to Billy the Kid, but it seemed funny that this entire gang would be sporting them.

The riders all jumped from their horses, and Jones immediately noticed something else about them. As they closed in, they didn't run so much as bounce from one rock to another, firing their pistols at the men from the wagon. Jones had never witnessed such gaits. The wagon driver, who appeared at this distance to be sporting an Indian headband, fired back, as did one of the men who had taken cover.

The attackers seemed to be using something like those newfangled Browning semi-automatics that Jones had heard about and seen once. Jones preferred the relative simplicity of his Colt six-shooter, and his hand brushed its walnut handle as he considered whether to take a hand in the business below. It was obvious which side the odds favored, but he didn't know what the battle was all about. He had almost decided to stay neutral when one of the bowler-hatted attackers glanced up and spotted him, and immediately fired off a couple shots in his direction.

One of the bullets whined off a rock behind him, and Jones slid off his horse and pulled Dusty back from the edge. That changed things. It was obvious now which faction didn't want to leave any witnesses.

He reached for his pistol again, but changed his mind and pulled his long 1874-pattern Sharps from its saddle scabbard instead. He could only fire one shot before having to reload, but he knew its range and accuracy could top anything that anybody was using below. If it would stop a charging buffalo, it ought to stop about anything. A Texan named Billy Dixon used one that effectively ended a Comanche siege at Adobe Wells in '74 by downing an attacker at a distance later measured at 1,500 yards. It was the most powerful weapon Jones had ever handled.

When Jones peered over the ridge again, he saw the bowler-hatted gunman who had targeted him bouncing up the incline in his direction. Another bullet buzzed over his head and ricocheted off the rock in back once more. Jones pulled back the hammer on his Sharps and targeted the ground just ahead of the approaching attacker. The bullet plowed up dirt inches from the man's feet.

It didn't discourage him a bit. He not only kept firing, but kept bounding upward toward Jones as though he thought himself bullet-proof.

"Oo-kay," Jones whispered, ejecting the shell and inserting a new cartridge. He pulled the gun's rear trigger, which set the front one to go off at the slightest touch, and sighted on the determined gunman. As the man drew uncomfortably closer, Jones saw that he sported a huge black handlebar mustache, which was about all he could make of the face. He touched the hair trigger and the Sharps boomed again.

Instead of falling, the charging man seemed to disappear in a puff of yellow smoke. Jones rubbed his eyes, but could spot no sign of a body. He wrinkled his nose as he caught a whiff of something that smelled like rotten eggs.

Now two more of the bowler-sporting attackers were firing up at him, but the others were still shooting at the wagon and Jones saw a man who had been returning fire spin around and go down behind a rock. Jones reloaded and drew down on one of the pair pinging at him. Again, he was sure his shot went home but, instead of simply falling over, his target vanished before he could blink.

The rest of the bowlers, as Jones was starting to think of them, broke and ran back to where their horses waited, their running still looking more like long zigzag leaps across the rocky ground. They literally sprang onto their mounts and galloped out of sight beyond the ridge.

Jones returned the rifle to his saddle, and picked up his horse's reins. "Let's amble down there and see what all that was about, Dusty," he said.

He picked his way carefully down the side, leading the horse, until he reached the wagon—or whatever it was.

Up close, the conveyance and its cargo loomed above him like a ship's hull. The strange-looking freight appeared to be made of some light wood, maybe sixty feet long, and the metal rods along its sides seemed to be reaching for the sky. They attached to pipes wrapping around what looked like wheels along the side and disappearing into the cigar-shaped whatever-it-was. It had what looked like a rounded window in front and fish-like fins on its backside.

Jones was so mesmerized by the sight that he all but ignored the men who came scrambling from behind rocks and hurried toward him. Two of them supported a third man, a white-haired old-timer with a matching white mustache whose buckskin shirt was bloodied around the shoulder.

"I guess I didn't do such a good job of body-guarding," the wounded man said, grimacing at each move.

"Just sit here, Rance, until we see how bad it is," said one of the men helping him, an easterner from the look of him, with hair slicked down and suspenders over his white shirt.

"I know I hit at least one of those critters," Rance grumbled, sitting on the bottom of what seemed to be a stairway up into the thing being towed by the mules.

"So did I," said the man with the headband, whose Indian-like features went with it but who otherwise wore conventional range clothing. "But it did not stop him."

"Your gun stopped them," said the older man supporting Rance, who looked like a more mature version of the young easterner. "What were you using, anyway?"

"Let me ask you something first," Jones said. He motioned up at the hulk atop the wheeled platform, and his voice was more intense than he'd intended. "What in blue blazes is that?"

"Oh, that's an airship," said the younger man matter-of-factly. "At least, that's what it's supposed to be." He sounded frustrated. "If we could keep it in the air for longer than a few days."

Jones stared at him. "That thing . . . what? Flies?"

"Don't sound so shocked," the young man said rather defensively. "People have had things in the air for years. Ever hear of Thad Lowe? He had a whole corps of balloonists during the Civil War who made hundreds of tethered flights over battlefields for reconnaissance. Lincoln approved the idea himself. We've just mechanized it, taken it to the next step."

"The lad's right. We've actually been doing flights for months now," the older version of the easterner said. "The idea was to start in the western end of the country, in California, and fly back to New York where we'd done the schematics and fabricated the parts to ship out here by rail. It was going to be a fine demonstration!" He grimaced. "As you can see, we haven't gotten very far."

"We had to put it down near a brewery in Sacramento the first time out," said the younger. "Of all places! Everybody probably thinks the people who spoke with us were intoxicated and made up the encounter. But since then, it seemed like whenever we've had to stop and descend for adjustments, we've been attacked by one or more of those men in bowler hats. What you saw just now was the worst assault so far. I just hope we can get this entourage turned around so we can get back out of this canyon."

"But—are you really saying this thing . . . flies?" Jones repeated, his gaze still fixated on it.

"Sometimes. It'll fly again if we can get those sunheaters making enough steam to store and power the engines. But right now we've got to get Rance, here, to a doctor. I guess we'll have to cut out one of the mules . . ."

Jones pulled his eyes away from the towering mechanism, and automatically took charge of a situation he could understand. "Can you sit a saddle?" he asked the wounded old-timer, just as three more men emerged belatedly from the rocks, looking around carefully to make sure more gunmen in bowlers weren't lurking.

"I reckon, long as the mule don't jostle too much," the man said.

"We won't need a mule if I can catch one of those two horses the 'bowlers' left," Jones said. "Hang on." He swung up into his saddle and galloped off.

Five minutes later, he was back, leading a sorrel by the reins. "It's a funny-looking saddle," he said, nodding toward the short stirrups and wide rounded seat. "But I guess it'll work."

While they were adjusting the stirrups, the younger man introduced himself as Hiram Wilson, and the older man as his father, Willard. The Indian driver simply called himself Charlie, and the rest identified themselves as Walsh, Jackson and Boswell, all three of them easterners, judging by their clothing. Walsh and Jackson were dressed like the Wilsons, jackets and suspenders and loose trousers, while Boswell wore jodhpurs, a uniform-like coat with epaulettes on the shoulders, and a smirk which, to Jones, seemed out of place under the circumstances. Jones almost had to resist contrary impulses either to salute him or kick his rear.

None of them had seemed surprised at Hiram's claim that this conveyance flew. Jones assumed they had either seen it fly, or they were as crazy as Hiram.

Now he found himself stuck with escorting the old codger named Rance to the nearest town where they might find a doctor. The others obviously were not horsemen. Amarillo and Lubbock were likely too far a ride for the wounded man, but Childress was relatively close by, and that was where Jones was headed, anyway.

The father and son managed a makeshift bandage for Rance, and helped Jones boost him up into the saddle. "Don't exactly fit my behind," Rance grumbled, "but I guess it beats walking."

They started off, going at an easy pace so as not to bump the old-timer around too much. On the way, Jones tried to quiz him about the flying machine, but Rance was not feeling up to much conversation—or maybe he just didn't want to talk about it.

Their destination, the town of Childress, had come into being mainly because of the Fort Worth and Denver Railway, which also had built a hotel within its borders. Jones had been heading there to meet Robert Steele, a rail executive whom Jones had known when they were both Pinkertons and who now wanted to offer Jones a job guarding rail payrolls and passengers, according to his telegram. The James, Younger and Reno gangs were all history, but others like Butch Cassidy's bunch had continued sticking up trains ever since Butch had gotten out of state prison at Laramie.

It was nightfall when their horses dragged into Childress. The place seemed to have more churches than anything else, but Jones did locate a doctor and a livery stable. He left Rance with the former and their horses at the latter, then found a restaurant and settled in for a late dinner. Steele was supposed to have reserved a room for him at the Dwight Hotel, where they would get together when Steele arrived. The day's events would provide quite a story for him, Jones thought, even though Steele probably wouldn't believe it. Jones wasn't sure he believed all of it himself.

He had stepped out onto the street, trying to decide whether to call it a day or treat himself to a whiskey at a nearby saloon, when he was struck by how everybody around him was standing rooted in place and staring up at the night sky.

Jones looked up, too, and saw what he first took to be a shooting star. But this bright light was moving too slowly over the town to be that. As his eyes grew more accustomed to the blackness above, he could make out a dark shape behind the light, a shape not unlike a fat cigar, floating from west to east as he and everybody around him stared in silence.

Then it was gone.

He looked around at the others on the street and found they had also been struck dumb by the sight and, like himself, stood immobile—except for one. Jones spotted movement from the corner of his eye, and saw a short round man in a black coat and bowler hat running on short legs for a horse. He bounced, literally bounced, into the saddle, and the horse trotted down a side street in the direction the shadowy form overhead had taken.

Maybe he wouldn't tell Steele that funny little story, after all.

"None of my business," Jones murmured to himself. But sleep didn't come easily that night, even in the comfortable hotel bed.

TWO

A Gang of Look-alikes

The next morning, he stopped by the livery stable to check on his horse, with a plan to head to the doctor's office next to check on Rance. But he learned the man had arrived ahead of him, arm in a sling, and said he was riding to try and catch up with his friends at Belton.

"Durnedest-looking saddle I ever saw," the livery man said. "Looked like it was fixed to seat a ten-pin bowling ball, 'stead of a rider's behind."

Jones shrugged his shoulders and turned toward the restaurant for a meal and coffee. Once he'd ordered breakfast, he found his gaze fixated on a young woman at a corner table in earnest conversation with a perplexed-looking older gent in a dark suit. She had light brown hair, blue eyes and a flawless complexion although her cheeks were bright pink right now with agitation. She wore a long, light-blue dress which matched her eyes. When the cook brought his steak, scrambled eggs and coffee, Jones asked in a low voice who the two were.

"That's Judge Garvey," the cook told him. "Nearest thing we got to anyone with any authority. Her name's Mrs. Dunston, and I guess she's telling him the same crazy story she's been trying to tell everyone else for the past two weeks."

"What story is that?"

"Well, she's a widow—husband died last year in that twister that hit St. Louie, and she come out here to set up some kind of astro-something or other. Some kind of teley-scope for lookin' at stars, sort of like the one that Mars fella built over in Arizona three years back, only not as big, I guess. Anyway, she's been complaining of being hurrahed by a bunch of men, stealing her equipment and even taking pot shots at her. Some townsmen rode out to her place a time or two, but they never found nobody there."

"Astro-something? You talking about astronomy? An observatory?"

"That's it, yeah. Her husband had been one of those astro-something guys. Don't know why a pretty thing like her wants to stay out there by herself lookin' through a teley-scope all night." He gave Jones a man-to-man grin which Jones didn't return. "Maybe that's what got her imagination all het up. But don't get her started on women doing stuff like that, or you'll be hearing all about Miss Mitchell's Comet and how some German lady helped her brother find a new planet and I don't know what all. And then she'll start on women getting the vote in Wyoming and Idaho and Colorado, and Utah even electing a woman senator last year . . ."

"Who does she say the men are?" Jones interrupted.

"Well, she's got some funny ideas about that, too. Like they come from someplace real far off. I never did understand that part. Oh yeah, and they all dress in black, have big mustaches and wear bowler hats."

Jones almost spit out the coffee he'd just sipped.

"What's the matter, too hot? Better hold it by the handle. 'Course, lots of men around here got mustaches and wear bowlers, like that fellow over by their table."

Jones found his appetite largely replaced by curiosity, but he worked at the meal as he strained in vain to hear the conversation between Mrs. Dunston and the judge. All right, it was still none of his business, but that curiosity of his was piqued. Maybe it helped that the young widow was awfully easy on the eyes. Maybe it was how those two men yesterday had seemed to vanish. Maybe it was the rotund man in a black suit with a thick mustache and bowler hat to whom the cook had just referred, sitting even closer to the judge and the widow and holding a steaming cup of coffee in both hands but not drinking from it. The cup obviously wasn't too hot for him.

The Widow Dunston's back was to the man, and nobody else in the room was paying him any heed. But Jones could see the man's attention was totally on the conversation behind him, the way he cocked his head in that direction. And that gave Jones the chance to study the man while chewing absently on a steak which would otherwise have commanded his full attention. The bowler was pulled down so the man's eyes were shadowed, and the thick mustache concealed both his mouth and the bottom part of his nose. His face, behind it, looked rather more round than the average face. In fact, the man's entire body had a roundness to it. The black suit he wore appeared ordinary enough, including the black string tie and vest under the coat. Jones could not tell if the man was armed, but figured that was the way to bet.

Who were these bowlers, who looked so much alike? Members of some outlaw family, like the Jameses or Youngers or Daltons? But even the Earp brothers, who resembled each other so much that they would sometimes be mistaken for one another, hadn't looked as similar as these yahoos. Or, Jones wondered, was his imagination running away with him? Was this man, sitting calmly a few feet away huddling over that steaming coffee, really part of a gang of look-alikes chasing a flying machine across the country?

Jones had about decided that it was all too silly to be taken seriously. He changed his mind when the Widow Dunston stood up, seemingly exasperated by the judge's reaction to whatever she was trying to tell him, turned around to where the stranger was sitting, and screamed.

The man shot to his feet, so quickly that he actually left the ground, overturning the chair in which he'd been sitting. Now people were looking at him, and he didn't seem to like that a bit. He gave a hopping sort of leap toward the swinging doors leading outside. Without even thinking about it, Jones stuck out his leg and caught the man's ankles, sending him sprawling face down with a thunderous crash.

Bob Fitzsimmons had been right after he knocked out Jim Corbett in that championship prize fight in Nevada earlier this year: The bigger they are, the harder they fall, indeed.

But it had been like swinging his leg against two steel bars. Jones found himself limping when he went after the downed man and grabbed him from behind in a bear hug. The man's trunk felt more like a rigid barrel than flesh and blood. The man pushed himself to his feet and shook off Jones like a buffalo shedding a flea. With a single bound, he was through the swinging door and gone.

"That . . ." Mrs. Dunston had placed her hands on a table, as though to keep herself from falling over, and was addressing herself to Judge Garvey. ". . . was one of them!"

"Now, now, Mrs. Dunston," the judge said in placating tones, "he was simply sitting there. Your reaction probably unnerved him. You really must get hold of yourself, dear lady. Surely you can see that your story is just too fantastic . . ."

"Fantastic!" she snorted. Pushing herself upright from the table, she started toward the door but paused when she got to Jones. "I thank you, sir, for what you attempted to do. I'm glad to see there is one man in this town unafraid of these interlopers."

She started off again, but Jones touched her arm. "Mrs. Dunston," he said quietly, "I've run into these characters once before. It was a strange experience. But I have no idea who they are. Would you mind telling me what you know about them?"

Those clear blue eyes looked at him more appraisingly. Jones was suddenly glad he'd shaved that morning. Finally, she gave a dainty shrug. "Why not?" she said. "I suppose I've told everybody else who might listen. Come, let us get out of this place."

As they started out, Jones overheard the cook murmur quietly to himself, "Now why didn't I think of that approach?"

Standing on the wooden sidewalk outside, Jones introduced himself and learned that Mrs. Dunston's first name was Amy—and she made no mocking remarks when she learned that his was Alistair, which raised his opinion of her still more. "I ran into a bunch of these bowlers yesterday," he told her. "They were chasing . . ." He hesitated. ". . . Chasing a wagon."

"Bowlers," she said. "Yes, that is a good name for them." She made a little moue of distaste which Jones found appealing.

"They, ah, aren't from around here, are they?"

He received the full focus of her blue eyes. "You would be surprised. Mr. Jones, just what is your interest in all this?"

He thought, well, mainly you, ma'am, but said, "Curiosity." And then, he proceeded to tell her a story he would never have told the judge or any legal official for fear of getting arrested on his own say-so. "I shot them both," he concluded. "Self-defense, though it might be hard to prove without witnesses from that sky-coach thing. But there were no bodies. They just . . . disappeared." He hesitated again. "Look, I know this all sounds crazy as a bessie bug, but . . ."

She laid a hand on his arm, just as he had on hers earlier. "Not at all. See here, would you ride with me to my residence? It is about a mile from here. I will tell you some things even more unbelievable."

Amy had come to town in a buckboard drawn by a single roan mare. While she was untying the horse from a hitch rack in front of the judge's office (she had started out there, she explained, but quickly learned he was more often to be found in the saloon part of the restaurant), Jones scrawled a hasty note and left it with the hotel clerk for Steele who should arrive any time now. Then he walked quickly to the livery stable and saddled up Dusty. As they rode out of town side by side, Amy Dunston did indeed tell Jones about things even more unbelievable.

"It's not as strange as all that," she insisted, noting a reaction he couldn't quite conceal. "Did you happen to read any of that recent story about Mars by that British writer, Mr. Wells?"

"I'm afraid I don't get to Britain that often," Jones said.

"Nor I, but it was serialized in a New York magazine earlier this year. Probably unauthorized, but I happened to see a copy of the opening segment. It begins with astronomers seeing explosions on Mars, and then missiles containing creatures from that world landing here."

"But that's just a story! You're not asking me to believe the bowlers are from Mars, are you?"

"Of course not," she said, but after an awkward pause added, "I have reason to believe they are from Venus."

Oh, well, Venus, he thought. Sure, that's different. But he managed not to change expression this time.

Jones went through the next several hours, which included her fixing them lunch, followed by a tour of the little workshop where Amy had ground the lenses for her telescope and filled out dozens of notebooks on her researches, and finally the makeshift observatory structure itself, all with a vague feeling of unreality. He had always thought of himself as a practical man. He had quit buffalo-hunting when he realized the herds were becoming too decimated to make the dirty skinning work worthwhile. He had left the Pinkerton Detective Agency ("We never sleep") when he started getting union-busting assignments instead of hunting badmen. He hadn't sought any more peace officer jobs after serving in a couple towns where the main task came down to handling belligerent drunks. And he'd accumulated enough of a stake that he really didn't need to be a passenger train guard except that Steele had promised it would be interesting work.

But now, in the space of less than two days, he had encountered a supposed flying machine, shot it out with assailants who vanished in a puff of smoke, and been told that strange men in bowler hats were visitors from another planet.

Most surprising of all, he'd found himself enamored of a strange yet lovely and intimidatingly smart young widow whom he hardly knew. It had not exactly been a normal week. And then it became even less normal.

Jones had been about to ask why Amy thought the bowlers had been harassing her when the first shots rang out. They splintered the wooden walls of the observatory, and one of them clanged off the metal telescope. Jones shoved Amy down behind the instrument and then peered out through the slit in the building where the telescope protruded.

At least three bowlers stood out there, one on the porch of the little house where Amy had prepared lunch, one behind a water trough, and the third bouncing across a little garden toward the observatory. Jones had left Dusty, unsaddled, grazing on grass shaded by some nearby trees. The saddle along with his Sharps was on the porch of the house, and the big gun might as well be on the moon for all the good it would do now. Jones jerked his six-gun from its holster and fired three shots at the charging figure. The bullets seemed to jar him, but they didn't stop him or even slow him down.

His fourth shot blew the bowler hat off the attacker's head, which proved to be hairless. He glimpsed an almost round and immobile face, now covered only by the thick mustache. The figure was close enough now that Jones could see its little eyes, if that's what they were. They looked more like tiny red fireballs.

But the attacker did stop his charge. His bouncing gait took him back after his hat, which had skittered a good distance away. Jones sent his last bullet after him, then frantically knocked the shells out of his pistol's cylinder, grabbed more cartridges from loops in his gun belt and this time filled all six slots. Still, he realized these bullets were not going to get the job done.

"Amy, is there any other way out of here?" he asked, crouching beside her.

"No." To his surprise, she didn't seem particularly rattled at being shot at. "But there is a crawlspace underneath." She backed over to where he could now make out a trapdoor in the floor, gripped its sides and pulled it upward enough so she could scurry beneath it. Jones was right behind her.

Under other circumstances, Jones would have enjoyed their proximity as they crouched together in the dark, and he allowed himself a moment to wish matters were different. But the sounds above of more shots being fired and walls crashing in drove away such thoughts. The clatter of breakage seemed to go on forever but, afterward, Jones figured it couldn't have been more than five minutes.

He and Amy continued to lie perfectly still, long after the noise had ceased. Each knew exactly what the other was thinking—that the trio of invaders must be waiting for them to come crawling out of the wreckage.

THREE
Warnings

It was night when Jones finally put his shoulders to the trapdoor and tried to raise it. At first, it wouldn't budge. He exerted himself, and pushed gradually upward as the debris piled on top of the door slowly slid away. When it was wide enough to accommodate his upper body, he crawled out as quietly as he could considering the broken equipment and splintered wood over which he was moving.

Nobody shot at him. Nothing bounced up to confront him. Eventually, he turned back to help Amy out of the crawlspace.

An almost-full moon showed the observatory walls completely gone. So was the workshop where Amy had prepared her telescope and kept her notes. Her house looked untouched. Jones gave a soft whistle, repeated several times, and was finally rewarded by a soft whinny back in the trees.

He holstered his pistol and went to the horse. Amy's roan mare was there, too. At least the intruders hadn't bothered them.

"They finally got it done," Amy said, surveying the destruction. "All the evidence, such as it was. All the astronomical notes . . ."

"They probably think they got us, too," said Jones. "What do you mean, evidence?"

"I hadn't told you quite everything," she said.

Jones stared. "There's more?"

"I didn't think even you would believe it all. You still may not."

Jones wasn't sure he would, either. But he only said, "Tell me."

"When I said those creatures were from Venus, it was not merely a guess," she began. "One of them told me."

Jones had thought her earlier story the strangest he had ever heard. But now she topped it.

She claimed the Venus men, as she called them, had been on this world at least since the early 1800s. She asked Jones if he'd ever heard tales about a folklore character in England called Spring-Heeled Jack, because of his ability to make extraordinary leaps. The creature, or creatures, as she now believed, had been seen in London, Liverpool and even Scotland. At the time, she said, England was seen as the planet's leader in industry, and that's why the original interest of the Venus men had been focused there.

"But how could they have come here at all?" Jones asked. He wasn't sure how far away Venus was, but he knew horsepower wouldn't bridge the gap. She told him of a supposed meteor which exploded over West Virginia last March, its debris causing some damage around New Martinsville. That had been one of their craft, she said, perhaps the only one which did not make landfall safely.

Her husband had been an astronomer at Washington University in St. Louis, and was doing a study of such meteorites. He alone had raised the question of whether any of them could be other than natural phenomena. The Venus men learned of his work, and decided it could be dangerous to them.

"I do not know how, but they can influence weather," she said. "They created the tornadoes that ravaged that part of the country last year, when my husband was killed. The twister was aimed at him, specifically. They also caused an extraordinary heat wave throughout the northeastern part of the nation last year, for no other reason than to increase their own comfort a small amount. They badly want a warmer world than we have now." Her eyes blazed. "I asked that murderer why they didn't just make all the world warm if they could control the weather. He didn't answer me. I think whatever machines they brought that do this can't keep it up for long. I think they wasted all the power in their device when they killed my husband . . ." Registering his confusion, she took a deep breath. "I'm sorry. I've gotten ahead of myself."

Her husband had shared every aspect of his work with her, and she was determined not to let him die in vain or let his research be forgotten. She relocated to a relatively-unoccupied part of the biggest state in the union where viewing conditions were better. She had been unaware of the presence of the Venus men or that they had targeted her husband at that time—until they located her and one of them had actually warned her to stop her studies.

"He spoke to you?" Jones asked.

It did, she said, in a horribly-scratchy voice and in broken English. One night two months ago one of the bowlers had been waiting for her outside the observatory, its gun drawn. She spotted it in time, locked the door and took cover, but it stayed to deliver its warning. That was when she learned about the weather having been used as a device to eliminate her husband and his research. The creature shared information with her as if it made no difference what she knew. What she gathered was that the Venus men had bigger fish to fry right now and would leave her alone if she left them alone by not pursuing her late husband's theories. She supposed they realized that her murder would arouse townspeople to investigate. They no doubt assumed she would be too frightened to try and draw public attention to them.

"I guess they realized their mistake," she said, surveying the debris all around.

Amy had sought help in town, saying only that she was under duress from the bowlers. Telling the entire story would be playing into their hands, or whatever digits they had, and likely get her committed. She had not told anyone—until now. She knew no one but Jones, who had also encountered the creatures, would believe her.

"But what do they want? Why are they here?" Jones asked.

"Their own world is a runaway greenhouse," she said. "They can only survive there for perhaps another century in the protective enclaves they have constructed. They need a new home. But our world is too cool for them at present. They want our industry to take a direction where it will pump more wastes into the atmosphere, to heat it to the point where they can survive comfortably, but not to the extent that their world has gone."

She studied Jones' face with her intense blue-eyed gaze. "You probably think I'm quite mad."

"The funny part is I don't," Jones said. "But I wonder if you'd believe my story."

He told her about the supposed flying machine, and how he might have seen it passing over Childress the night before. She pressed for details. He added what he could recall about the conversation he'd had with the men aboard.

"Why, don't you see? That explains it!" she said. "That is why they thought it worthwhile to try and get me to stop voluntarily. They did not want to have to leave any of their number around to swat me down and clean up the mess afterward." Her mouth thinned in a grim line. "And that is also why they didn't wait us out—because they needed to concentrate their resources on your flying machine."

"It's not my machine," Jones said. "But why would they be so anxious to destroy it?"

"You said one of the fliers made reference to its being powered by sun-heaters! If that proves successful, it would mean a whole new approach to power generation, instead of the kind the Venus men hope we will use. Sun-heaters sound like they would not fill our atmosphere with the kinds of contaminants that would heat up our environment, don't you see?"

Jones wasn't sure he did, but he wasn't about to admit it. Better to stay quiet and be thought a fool than to speak and remove all doubt. He was, after all, a practical man.

"We must catch up with your sky-coach people," Amy said. "We must warn them."

"Now, hold on. If that thing really flies, we can't overhaul it on horseback." Actually, he wasn't so sure about that. For a flying machine, the sky-coach didn't seem to be generating much speed in its cross-country trek. "Besides, we don't know which way it's going. Well, generally east, but that's not enough."

"Think, Mr. Jones!" she urged. "Surely one of the men must have said something which would give you a clue."

Jones felt strangely moved by her faith in his powers of recollection. He replayed the conversation in his mind. "No," he said reluctantly, "nothing. At least, nothing they said . . ."

But he remembered what the stable-hand in Childress had mentioned about the old-timer. Rance had ridden off saying he would catch up with his friends in Belton. Maybe the craft had scheduled a maintenance stop there.

"Belton," he said. "That might be where they were headed."

"Oh dear," Amy said. "Belton is three or four hundred miles away. It would take forever on horseback."

"How about rail? I know someone who should be in Childress by now and who has some pull with the Fort Worth and Denver Railway . . ."

Robert Steele had indeed arrived, and was disappointed that Jones wasn't taking him up on his job offer, at least not right away. Jones cited a family emergency. "I didn't know you still had any family," a dubious-sounding Steele said. Well, not exactly family, but a close friend, Jones amended.

And he needed to take another passenger. Amy Dunston had made it clear that she would not be left behind.

"Well, we've known each other a long time," Steele said. "So I'm not going to ask the obvious questions. But whenever you've finished whatever you're doing now, maybe you'll tell me more. And maybe you'll still be interested in my proposition."

Jones arranged an extended stay at the livery stable for their horses, taking his Sharps and its scabbard off his saddle, and soon they were on their way to Belton, passengers on a non-passenger train where they had to ride in the mail car, but it would get them there the next day.

Knowing Amy had been an easterner, Jones was surprised at how easily she adapted to the conditions. She charmed the straight-laced courier in the mail car despite his initial misgivings about the proprieties of a man and woman traveling this way (Steele had indeed pulled some strings), and she managed to nap more than Jones had with only a mail sack for a pillow.

Amy had changed into horseback riding clothes before they left her home, her dress having been in ruined by the debris they'd had to climb through. Jones had made a quick change at his hotel back in Childress. He hoped they didn't look too disreputable after a night and part of a day roughing it, when he finally jumped down from the mail car and turned to lift Amy down—the first time, he realized, he had actually touched her in that way. She didn't seem to mind.

Unfortunately, the railroad had bypassed Belton when it was constructed, and they had to find a wagon and driver to hire to take them the rest of the way. When they finally got there, Jones again had the pleasure of lifting her down.

"Now what?" she said.

"Now," Jones said, hefting his rifle scabbard, "we start asking around if anyone has seen any strange sights in the sky."

It didn't take long to get results—but not the results they were seeking. Their inquiries drew blank stares, head shakes or derisive and sometimes off-color comments, until a man on the street walked deliberately up to them.

He was a skinny guy with a slim mustache and a belt supporting two holstered pistols. To Jones, he looked like someone who had just stepped out of a dime novel—except for a pallor not usual in this part of the country. He had swaggered toward them while they stood conferring on the porch of a hotel building, and jabbed a long finger into Jones' chest.

"I know you!" the man said. "I'm givin' you and your woman here just thirty minutes to get out of town, while you can still walk."

It was all Jones could do to keep from laughing, so scripted did it sound. "What are you going to do, cut off our legs?" he said.

The man's face reddened. "You're carryin' a rifle and wearin' a six-gun. Go for it."

"Why?" Jones asked mildly.

"Why?" The man was becoming really upset. Jones wasn't playing the game. "I'm givin' you a chance to draw, mister. But I'm not gonna wait forever . . . "

Jones had been holding his arms out away from his sides, as he stepped closer. And then he grasped the rifle scabbard and swung the butt of the Sharps across the man's face, staggering him. He sunk his left fist into the man's stomach, doubling him over, and then brought up a knee into his face, putting him flat on his back.

While the man was still dazed, Jones deftly removed his pistols. He glanced over at Amy. To his surprise, he saw that she had produced a tiny derringer from somewhere and was pointing it straight at the prone stranger.

She made it vanish as quickly as she had produced it. "That was just in case," she said.

A few bystanders started to gather around them and the prone figure on the ground. "What's going on?" demanded a lanky man in a dark suit, with a deputy sheriff's badge peeking from under his coat.

While Jones was wondering whether the deputy would believe the truth, that the man had tried to force him into a gunfight, Amy pre-empted him again. "This man attempted to rob us," she said. "We want to prefer charges against him."

"Looks like your man here handled the situation," drawled the deputy. "But we'll haul him down to the office and get this straightened out. You, and you," he said, jerking his thumb toward a pair of onlookers, "pick him up and follow us."

By the time the man came around, he was propped up in a chair with Jones, Amy, the deputy and another officer all staring down at him. He started to get up but the deputy put a restraining hand on his shoulder.

"Why did you try to stick these people up?" the deputy asked.

"What? I didn't . . . what are you . . . " The man attempted several responses before a coherent one came out. "I didn't do no such a thing!"

"Then what did you do?" Amy asked mildly.

Jones could almost see the conflicts in the man's thoughts. How could he say he had tried to force a gunfight? Where had this robbery accusation come from? How was he going to get out of this?

Amy provided him an alternative. "Tell us who put you up to this, and we will drop the charges," she said.

Now it was the deputy's turn to look perplexed. Before he could raise a question, Jones spoke up. "Come on, speak up. Would you rather go to prison?"

"No! Gawd, no," the man said, and all at once Jones knew where he had lost his tan. He'd already been in prison somewhere, and it hadn't been a positive experience. "All right, okay, I don't know his name, but he was an easterner. Gave me fifty dollars and promised a hundred more if I got you two out of the way."

"How did you know who we were?" Jones asked.

"The hombre described you perfectly. The lady, not as well, but he said you'd be together. He was in kind of a hurry. Said he had to get back somewhere with some provisions he was buying . . . "

"Describe him," Amy said. "Was he wearing a bowler hat?"

"No, nothin' like that. An easterner, like I said. Slicked-back hair, dark, sideburns, riding britches . . ."

The lanky deputy had had enough. "What are you all talking about? Start making sense, fellow."

Behind him, Jones jerked his head toward the door and Amy quietly backed outside with him. They didn't talk until they had gone around several corners and were pretty sure the deputy couldn't follow them, even if he was inclined to do so.

"They're here somewhere. They're waiting for that machine, that sky-coach," Amy said.

"So all we have to do is wait, too. And stay out of the deputy's way. I can't answer his questions any better than their hired gun could."

"They have a better grasp of our culture than I imagined," Amy said. "And they are still looking for the simplest and least revealing way to handle us."

"But you think they created a tornado just to get at your husband. That isn't exactly being inconspicuous."

"Who's going to be suspicious of a killer tornado? Or an aggressive gunman? I'm just grateful their weather machine must not be working, or we'd be running from something more than a simple-minded ruffian. We must find a place where we can remain away from that deputy, and the gunman if he's released, and whoever hired him. Not to mention the bowlers, if they're here. That has to be our first priority."

In the end, they decided to get out of Belton altogether, but not far. Jones rented a pair of bay horses from a local livery, asked about nearby accommodations, and they ended up riding about ten miles southwest to a village called Salado. There was an awkward moment when the clerk at the Stagecoach Inn assumed they were husband and wife and started to assign them a single room. He looked puzzled when Jones insisted on separate rooms, but didn't argue. Jones paid for several days from a bankroll not as large as when he had started this venture. He might end up having to take Steele up on that job offer yet.

Both their rooms were on the second floor. They took turns for the next two days, and nights, watching the skies from its railed balcony. "Maybe we've missed it altogether?" Amy wondered on the morning of the third day.

"I don't think so." Jones had not told her about the broad-bottomed saddle he had seen at the Belton livery, or about the stable owner who said a white-haired man with a handlebar mustache had sold it for "a little walkin'-around money while he waited for some friends." It must have been old Rance, the group's erstwhile bodyguard. There was no mistaking that saddle, and Jones couldn't blame Rance for unloading when he found someone gullible enough to pay something for it. "I've never seen one just like it," the owner added. "It's gotta be a rarity. You interested in buyin' it, mister?"

Not unless I had a bowling ball for a butt, Jones thought. But it meant Rance no longer needed even a misshapen saddle and that Belton was as far as he'd needed to ride. Still, Jones didn't want to get Amy's hopes up. It could also mean that the sky-coach had already rendezvoused with Rance and was on its way elsewhere.

Looking at Amy, Jones had no idea how she could still appear so fresh. He had managed to wash out his shirt and socks and underwear once with a basin of water during one of his breaks from watching, and he assumed she must have, too, since neither of them had brought along a change of clothing. But he decided that maybe the wear and tear just looked better on her. Smelled better, too.

They learned that the place where they were staying was thirty-six years old and had played host to quite a few celebrated tenants—George Custer, Robert E. Lee and Jesse James, among others. But Jones knew nobody had ever stayed here for the same reasons as him and Amy.

FOUR
Down in Flames

The stars had started to appear in the darkening sky that evening when Amy called to him from the balcony. When he stepped from his room, she pointed silently up at a bright light moving across the night.

"That's it," Jones breathed.

In a matter of minutes, he had paid their bill, saddled and bridled their horses, and they were galloping after the moving light toward Belton.

Trusting the rented horse to see any obstacles ahead, Jones kept an eye on the apparition in the night sky. When he squinted, he could make out smaller lights of different colors along its length. Lanterns? Or did those lights have to do with the sun-heaters Hiram Wilson had mentioned? And how was sun-power managing to function at night? As his eyes grew more accustomed to the darkness, Jones thought he saw something like a sail billowing out over the cigar-shape.

"We're gaining on it," Amy said. "It looks like it's moving downward."

The buildings of the town were coming up fast. Jones and Amy slowed their horses as they followed the path of the air-coach along the streets of Belton. Jones decided they needn't worry about being pulled aside by that deputy for further questioning, because not a single person along the streets was looking at them. Everyone was looking up, pointing and yelling.

Jones thought he could hear some of the air-coach crew yelling back from up there, but whatever they were saying was lost in the wind. The air-coach was definitely coming lower, though. People along the streets ran to try and keep up, but none of them were mounted. Jones and Amy pulled ahead of them on their horses.

In less than fifteen minutes, they emerged far on the other side of Belton, with only a handful of the residents on foot still trying to keep up. Even those finally dropped away. Jones and Amy continued out onto the flatlands, as the shadowy form of the air-coach finally touched down, seemed to bounce, and then settled to a stop.

The huge foreign object suddenly registered with Amy's horse, which spun in the opposite direction and left Amy minus one stirrup and hanging off one side. Jones' bay decided that Amy's horse probably knew something he didn't, and began rearing and plunging as well. Jones found himself wishing for Dusty, who was waiting back in Childress for him. Knowing he wouldn't be able to control the rented horse, he kicked his feet free of the stirrups, grabbed the rifle scabbard and pulled it off the saddle, and swung to the ground before he could be thrown there. He managed to catch Amy as she came loose from her saddle.

The two bays had turned back toward Belton and were galloping away, kicking their feet as they sped off. Jones figured they would be back at their livery stable inside of ten minutes.

Amy pushed her hat back and looked up at him. "Thanks," she said. "But you can put me down now."

Startled, he did—albeit he wished he didn't have to—and they ran toward the shadowy form looming up ahead of them. And they found they had company.

"Wait for me!" came a voice behind them. Rance, one arm waving and the other in a sling, came after them at a slower pace. "We got to get aboard and get the hell out of here!"

Jones wondered at the urgency but then saw the rounded shadowy forms bouncing along the ground some distance behind Rance.

"Oh . . . my . . . God," he breathed, grabbing Amy's arm and propelling her toward the sky-coach. He risked another glance back. He couldn't be certain how many bowlers pursued them, but it seemed like more every minute, leaping impossible distances over the plain as if a swarm of oversized, well-manicured fleas bore down on them. It was simultaneously the silliest and most frightening thing Jones had ever seen.

"Ropes! Throw down the ropes," Rance yelled up to the crew. Jones spotted the Willards and three other men peering down at them. Then a pair of rope ladders and one long rope knotted at intervals came snaking down the sides of the monstrosity.

"Go on, Amy. Start climbing," Jones said, turning her toward one of the rope ladders. Rance began scrambling up the other, grimacing when he had to use his slinged arm to pull himself along. Jones loosened the strap on the rifle scabbard and hung it around his shoulder so as to have both arms free. Then he grabbed onto the knotted rope and started hauling himself up. He would have preferred one of the ladders, but figured Amy and Rance would need them more.

He regretted it about halfway up, as the strain began to tell on his hands and arms. "Hurry up!" came a voice Jones recognized as Hiram Wilson's. "They're coming!"

Thus encouraged, Jones made it the rest of the way and followed Amy over the side onto the narrow deck of the sky-coach. Then, his arms still shaking from the strain, he joined Wilson in pulling up the rope and the ladders. "Where's Charlie and the wagon?" the man Jones remembered as Boswell demanded of Rance.

"Charlie ain't here. Had to run off with the wagon to keep clear of those guys with the bowlers," Rance said. "I dropped off and hid near where we figured you'd planned to come down. But they must've figured out where, too. Don't ask me how."

A scattering of shots sounded below. Jones could hear plunks of bullets hitting the wooden rails. He pushed Amy down and cocked the Sharps. It was too dark to see much, but he began firing back, ejecting shells and firing again at the leaping shapes. When he fired for the fifth time, he was rewarded with what looked like a sulfurous yellow explosion.

"You got one!" Wilson said.

Jones turned around and gripped the easterner's shoulder. "Listen. If this thing can still fly, it had better fly now!"

Hiram Wilson hesitated. "Well, it could, but we need to vent some steam first because we generated too much reserve with the sun-heaters today. Otherwise, we'd be risking a catastrophic explosion . . ."

Both of them and the others crouched behind them heard the thud as one of the bowlers actually made a leap high enough to grab onto the rail. A round face under the bowler popped up inches from Jones' own face. It was too close to aim the rifle, so Jones slammed the butt right between the glowing red eyes. The blow echoed as though striking something metallic and hollow, and the shock reverberated up Jones' arms, but the creature lost its grip and fell.

"Fly! Now," Jones said.

"But it will be very dangerous . . ."

Amy seized Wilson's jacket in both hands and shook him with a ferocity Jones could hardly believe from such a slender form. "Right now!" she said.

Without another word, Wilson jumped back to what, in the glow cast by the fiery lights along the sides of the craft, appeared to be a set of levers. His father, Walsh and Jackson took stations alongside him, pulling on ropes that raised what looked like sails, jerking handles that activated pinwheels of radiance where the various lights were located. Boswell started to say something which sounded like a protest. "Shut up and pull," Walsh told him. With seeming reluctance, Boswell grabbed onto the rope on which Walsh was hauling.

Jones felt a lurch beneath his feet. Boswell fell against him, nearly sending him over the rail. He lost his grip on the Sharps, which slid over the side and disappeared below.

"Oh, great," he murmured, shoving Boswell away from him. He jerked his Colt from its holster as another round face appeared in silhouette at the rail, and fanned the hammer as he held back the trigger sending six shots toward it at point-blank range. The bullets hammered against the face, and the would-be boarder lost its grip and fell away.

The craft rose, silently except for hissing noises coming from the spinning light sources. Gripping the rail with both hands, Jones glanced down at the land falling away and saw more black forms bounding high into the air but now falling short.

"Where to?" Hiram Wilson called out.

"Kingdom come!" Jones shouted back.

Then he heard Amy yell, "That voice! I'd know it any-where!" followed by the sounds of a scuffle.

In the flickering light from the propulsion mecha-nisms, he could see her struggling over something square and black-metallic which Boswell was clutching in his hand.

"He's talking to them!" she said to Jones.

Jones couldn't quite accept that, but he could accept that Boswell was pushing Amy around and that was all that was necessary for him to act. It took only one blow to the point of the chin to put Boswell down onto the deck, all but unconscious. The black box dropped from his hand and Amy scooped it up.

"There! That should turn it off," she said, doing something with a tiny switch on its side. Hiram Wilson and his father were fully occupied with the air-coach, but Walsh and Jackson lunged forward as though to re-strain Jones before he could strike their comrade again. "Are you mad?" Jackson demanded. "What do you think you're doing?"

"If not mad, I am certainly highly irritated," Amy shot back, holding up the box. "This is how those creatures have been tracking you across the country. This man," she gestured at Boswell, "has been working for them."

"Are you saying that device is some sort of telephone?" Walsh said. "But it has no wires attached . . ."

"Have you not heard of the work of Tesla, and Mar-coni, in just the past year?" she said. "Your enemies have obviously made a huge leap in the development of wire-less communication."

Jackson stared at her. "My dear lady, don't be absurd. Nobody has accomplished anything like that . . ."

Instead of replying, Amy flipped the tiny switch back on and held the device up to Jackson's ear. Even Jones could hear, if barely, the scratchy voice that emanated from it. "Boss-will! Boss-will! Are you there? . . ." She cut the switch off again.

Jackson turned to Walsh, eyes wide. "Remarkable," he said. He looked down at Boswell, who was showing signs of life once more. "But why?"

Jones grasped the man's jacket lapels and hauled him roughly to his feet. He pulled him to the rail's edge, where the sight of the distant surface below almost made him dizzy and seemed to have the same effect on Boswell. "You have to be the one who hired that gunman back in Belton," Jones said. "Now you can either answer my questions or join your friends down there."

"No! Wait!" Boswell said, all of his arrogance having evaporated.

"I say, hold on there, you can't do that . . . " Jackson began, but Jones ignored him.

"You can't escape them!" Boswell began spouting. "I don't know what nation they represent, but their science is as far beyond ours as our own is beyond the Tasmanian aborigines. One of them approached me shortly after I started working with you and the Wilsons on this very craft. He said it had to be stopped! Its motive power would take us in the wrong direction . . . "

"The wrong direction for them," Amy said.

Hiram Wilson was still working his levers but now most of his attention was on Boswell. "How could you?" he demanded. "What we're trying here could advance civilization by leaps and bounds, and you want to help someone stop it?"

"You don't understand! I was trying to save all your lives. They're right here. Their enclave is here."

Hiram went wide-eyed, quivering with indignation. "You! You planned this route! You steered us right to them!"

Yet Boswell went on as if the younger man hadn't spoken. "It doesn't matter what we do. The end is close by now. They have the ability to bring this craft down in flames! And they told me, if we got this far, that is exactly what they would do."

"You mean their headquarters, their base of operations, is nearby?" Amy asked.

"Yes! We are getting closer every minute! If we don't cooperate, they will destroy us utterly . . ."

"Unless we put down soon and let off some steam," Willard Wilson said, "they won't have to." He pointed at the glowing lights along this side of the craft. Even Jones could see that they had become almost too bright to look at.

Amy spoke to Boswell. "Could you guide this machine by yourself to their enclave? Is that possible?"

"Of course." Some of Boswell's haughtiness had returned. "As I said, they are very close now . . ."

"Step back." Amy's voice cracked like a whip, and Jones saw that she had produced the derringer once more—and was pointing it at him, and the other crew members. "Step away from the controls and let Mr. Boswell take over."

"Amy," Jones said. "What are you doing?"

"Lower the ladders," she commanded. "I mean it. Throw them over the side or I will shoot."

"Hold on!" Hiram Wilson said. "You can't do this . . ."

Her little gun spat flame and a hole appeared in a wooden support structure inches from Wilson's right ear. "Do it!" she said. "Mr. Boswell, take your station. Here, take your communication device. Tell them we have hijacked the craft and are bringing it to them. Then bring us lower so these others can descend to the ground."

"With pleasure, Mrs. Dunston. You have chosen wisely." He began manipulating the levers, and the craft seemed to slow. Soon it was almost skimming the ground. "These people will reward you as they have already pledged to reward me—not with mere money, but power. They will be the eventual rulers of this young nation, perhaps the entire world . . . "

"All right, the rest of you," Amy said, gesturing with the derringer. "Over the side and down. Quickly now!"

Jackson hesitated. "That pistol only holds two cartridges, ma'am. You can't shoot us all . . . "

She pointed it at his face. "Do you want it to be you, sir?"

Jackson moved quickly to the ladder. Walsh, Rance and the two Wilsons followed. Amy watched as they went down a rung at a time, and turned back only when she saw they had all landed running or sprawling below.

"You too, Mr. Jones," she said. "Hurry "

Jones shook his head. "I'm sticking."

She stared. He bet that she had this exchange already written in her head, how it was supposed to go, but he wasn't going to play along. "But you've got to go," she finally said. "I have to do this . . . "

Jones folded his arms across his chest, which proved more difficult than he'd anticipated on the swaying deck. "I'm staying with you," he said. "Don't you think I know what's going on?"

"We're almost there," Boswell proclaimed, hauling back on one of the levers and further slowing the sky-coach. "See that big lump ahead? That's it."

They saw an enormous gray shape resembling the top half of an egg. In the semi-darkness, it appeared featureless. Ignoring Amy's derringer, Jones pulled out his own pistol and clunked Boswell over the head. The man folded. Jones holstered the weapon, caught him, threw his limp form across the rail, grabbed his feet and flipped him over the side.

"You might have killed him!" Amy said.

"And what were you going to do with him?" Jones asked, ramming forward the lever on which Boswell had been easing up. The craft picked up speed. Jones caught Amy around the waist, climbed to the rail and jumped.

Amy's scream was cut off when they jerked to a stop just before they would have plowed into the ground. Jones gave a grunt, then released her to fall the last few yards and let go of the knotted rope he'd snatched just before he leapt.

He rolled on the ground but came up in time to see the back of the sky-coach accelerating even more. Amy knelt on the ground close by. Jones ran toward her and bore her to the ground, sprawling on top of her as the explosion erupted. He felt a searing heat on his back, but it passed quickly.

After a moment, he scrambled to his feet and helped Amy to hers. "You knew what I was going to do," she said breathlessly.

"Yeah," Jones grinned. "But I didn't see any reason why you should go up with it."

"I did," she said, and for a moment her lovely face was overtaken by grief so profound it broke his heart to see it. Her gaze focused somewhere far away, and Jones understood immediately who she must be seeing.

He watched the smoking crater where that vague half-globe had been minutes ago. When he turned to her again, there were tears on her cheeks, but she smiled at him.

He said, "It's going to be a long walk back to Belton. Think you can make it?"

She gave a shaky laugh. "That will be the least of the exertions I've been through lately," she said. "I wonder . . ."

"Wonder what?" Jones prompted.

"Whether the Wilsons or anyone will be able to build anything like that sky-coach again. That was what the bowlers wanted to stop. They might have gotten exactly what they wanted after all."

Jones had no answer to that. Finally, he reached down and took her hand, and began their trek back they way they had come. They did not encounter any of the others, who were apparently well ahead of them. They did not find Boswell, or his body.

They had been walking for almost an hour before Amy spoke again.

"I wonder how many of them are left," she asked.

"I don't know," Jones said. Then he added, "But I'm glad you're an astronomer."

"Glad? Why?"

He held her hand more tightly as they walked side by side. "Because I think you and I will be watching the skies every night for the rest of our lives."

A Note from the Authors

L ife on Venus? The idea of Venus being a lush jungle world as depicted by writers from Burroughs to Bradbury pretty much died even before the first space probes from Earth reached our "twin sister." Carl Sagan wrote about scientists who had already figured out the runaway greenhouse effect that helped make Venus a hellhole and opined, because of the warning it should bring to us on our own planet (not that it has), their faces should be honored on postage stamps.

But . . . life on Venus? Just suppose . . .

UFO enthusiasts often list the "airships" of the late 1800s as precursors to our "flying saucer" craze that began in 1947 and never quit (remember the separating "saucer" section of the Enterprise from "The Next Generation" pilot? That configuration remains). Shalon Hurlbert even came up with a concept for Mike on how such an airship might have worked, based on the technology of the late 19th century. Some have even found accounts where people claimed to have talked to those pre-heavier-than-air ship pilots, some of whom gave hints of names and backgrounds (on which we've elaborated). That's probably as much of a stretch as the goober in some swamp who is chosen as the contact human by highly-advanced extraterrestrials.

But . . . early airships? Just suppose . . .

When Mike, Paul, and Mike's wife, Anita, began exploring the period around that time, all kinds of urban legends began popping up. Spring-heeled Jack? H. G. Wells' invention of what would become the major tropes of science fiction? The decline of the Wild West? Could we pull these elements together to come up with what Mike called a steampunk western?

Suppose? Just suppose . . .

— Paul Dellinger and Mike Allen, September 2014

About the Authors

Paul Dellinger spent four decades as a newspaper reporter. A native Virginian, he graduated from Roanoke College, spent three years in the U.S. Army as an information specialist (where he wrote a musical comedy performed at the West Point Service Club), created a tongue-in-cheek radio serial with Craig Allison which ran for two years on a Wytheville, Va., station ("The Adventures of Hap Hazard"), had a play produced in 1970 at Barter Theater, The State Theater of Virginia ("Rat Race," based on his first published short story), co-authored a book with Danny B. Gordon on the surprising effects of a UFO flap on residents of a small town (*Don't Look Up!*), and wrote a series of articles in specialty publications on vintage B-westerns and science fiction movies. He and his wife, Maxine, have two grown children, Mark and Katie, and two grandchildren, Grace and Emma. He lives in Wytheville, pursuing activities from horseback riding with his wife to local library volunteer activities.

On weekdays, Mike Allen writes the arts column for the daily newspaper in Roanoke, Va. Most of the rest of his time he devotes to writing, editing, and publishing. His first novel, a dark fantasy called *The Black Fire Concerto*, appeared in 2013, and he's written a sequel, The Ghoulmaker's Aria, that's in the revision stage.

He raised more than $20,000 through two Kickstarter campaigns to revive his anthology series dedicated to boundary-blurring work, *Clockwork Phoenix*. He also edits and publishes *Mythic Delirium*, which began in 1998 as a poetry journal; another Kickstarter campaign in 2013 rebooted it as a digital publication for poetry and fiction. 2014 saw the release of his sixth poetry collection, *Hungry Constellations*, and his first collection of short fiction, *Unseaming*. He'll release a new collection, *The Spider Tapestries*, and a new anthology, *Clockwork Phoenix 5*, in 2016.

He receives a ton of help with all this editing from his wife, artist and horticulturalist Anita Allen. Their pets, Loki (canine) and Persephone and Pandora (feline) provide distractions. You can follow Mike's exploits as a writer at descentintolight.com, as an editor at mythicdelirium.com, and all at once on Twitter at @mythicdelirium.